Prologue

Depsy Hospital closed fifty years ago, and the perfect spot to destroy my victims. Raven Marett, Sky Masters, Hazel Cras, Miranda Skew, Lexi Skew, Dexter Deter, Carmen Lough, Dan Lowell, Carter Powell, and Mason Defain. Soon I will be the only one alive on that list, and I will be accepted by the ones I respect most.

"You have everything sent out and ready, correct?" The Cult leader questions.

"Yes, they all should arrive at the hospital soon, all I need is for you to keep missing person reports from reaching the police," I say with determination in my voice.

"Will do, now go and may you not be found out," he says shooing me out of the room and shutting the door.

I arrive at the Hospital and I see all of my victims, time for the fun to begin

Chapter 1.R

"So the first one to arrive, great," I say to myself looking at the creepy hospital in front of me.

"I have arrived!" someone boldly states from behind me, "The one, The only Carmen Lough, The best person you'll ever meet." The girl, Carmen, looks at me with a huge smile on her face, seeming unaffected by the terrifying hospital looming over us.

"Hi I'm Raven," I say extending my hand out for a handshake. Carmen grabs my hand and pulls me into a crushing hug. "Can't breath," I barely breath out

"Oh, sorry," Carmen said scratching her neck awkwardly, "Anyways as I said before I'm Carmen, and I'm one-hundred percent sure I will be the best person you'll ever meet." Carmen smiles at me, but her smile doesn't last long when she turns around to look at the hospital. "So this is where we were suppose to go right, it doesn't look all too safe."

"Yeah I guess this is the place, it's where google maps took me," I say checking my phone again just to make sure. Other people start arriving one by one, none of them really communicating with one another .

"Welcome thank you all for coming to play some games with me," A deep obviously altered voice says from somewhere undetectable, "You all should enter the hospital or I might have to show everyone how I feel about people who don't listen." The voice caught all of us us all off guard ,but once It was done speaking we all scurried into the hospital.

"Creepy in here ain't it," Dexter, a boy that seems very sporty, said with a slight country accent,"I wonder if there is any food around here."

"Probably not," Carter said with the most boring voice. Carter was the last person to arrive, and from what I can tell she either has the personality of a sheet of paper or is really bad at showing emotions.

"Can we just get this over with, the beanie that I ordered is arriving tonight," Hazel said while looking at her phone.

"Yeah, I like have a party to go to," Miranda said also looking at her phone. Her younger sister, Lexi, was nodding furiously after she finished talking

"I don't know if we should leave, the voice said they would show how they feel about people not listening to them," Dan said stuttering on every other word. I nodded my head showing that I agreed with him.

"That is true we don't know what they mean," Sky said in a monotone voice, but still you could tell he cared, somewhat.

"Well let's get the party started, there should be a bowl in front of you," the voice from earlier said, "there is 10 of each of your names in the bowl, Pick one and say the name on the paper, I will explain what's going on once everyone is done."

I went up first and pulled a name, "Sky Masters," I said showing everyone the paper.

"Miranda Skew, " Hazel said.

"Dexter Deter," Sky stated.

"Miranda Skew," Lexi squawked out.

"Sky Masters," Miranda said while chewing a huge wad of gum.

"Miranda Skew," Mason said.

"Dan Lowell," Dan stuttered out his own name.

"Raven Marett," Carter mumbled staring at her hands.

"Miranda Skew," Dexter said while munching on a protein bar.

"Sky Masters," Carmen loudly stated.

"So Miranda Skew and Sky Masters, what will they receive, a chance to die in our very first game," The voice stated.

"What!" I shouted, "This is not right, this is horrible, I'm calling the cops." I try to turn on my phone but it explodes in my hand. "What the heck!" "If anyone tries to call the cops their phone will explode and If you try to leave you will die, ok," the voice stated harshly, "Now Sky and Miranda I want both of you to pick someone to help you escape the gas chamber you will be put in."

"Raven I want you to help me," Sky said almost instantly after the voice stopped.

"Uhh… I want Hazel to help me," Miranda said with a shaking voice filled with fear.

"Go through the door that just opened and I will Instruct you further, as for the rest of you I would advise you to socialize with each other;" The voice said. Sky, Miranda, Hazel, and I all went through the door, It slammed shut after we entered. "Hazel and Raven you will have to solve three logic puzzles, the first person to finish all three will save the person they are trying to save, now Sky and Miranda enter the pods in front of you and the game will start."

Sky and Miranda entered the two pods and as the doors closed a light lit up and there was a table with the first puzzle. A word search, good thing I'm good at these things. I found the three words, Yellow, Noxious, and Fumes quickly, and a light turned on over a table with the second puzzle. A riddle, This old one runs forever, but never moves at all. He has not lungs nor throat, but still a mighty roaring call. What is it?, it takes me a bit to figure out, but I figure out the answer is a waterfall. The last light turns on right next to Sky's chamber and that is where the final puzzle lies.

" Hurry up Hazel, I don't want to die, please," Miranda said with desperation.

"I'm trying," Hazel growls while looking down at the puzzle

"Doesn't sound like it," Miranda snapped, and Hazel just looks up and stares at her with a fire in her eyes for a few seconds and then finished the first puzzle once she looked down. I looked down at the last table and there was three buttons all saying push me, but they were all different colors, black, yellow, and blue. Walls erect around me, and I remember that the color of Sky's pod was blue, Miranda's was black, and the cross word puzzle said yellow noxious fumes. I hit the black hoping that it saves Sky and sadly kills off Miranda. The walls fall down and all the lights turn off leaving me and the others in pitch black. The lights of the two pods turn on, you could cut the suspense with a knife. A few seconds later yellow gas starts pouring into Miranda's chamber.

"No I don't want to die, NOOOOOO!!!!" And with her shrill screams still ringing in my ear I see her fall limp on the glass of the chamber. Sky's chamber opened and he ran out and crushed me in his embrace.

Chapter 2.S

I crushed him in my embrace, happy that I chose him to fight for my life. I knew he was logical and seemed to be the strongest willed out of the people here. "Thank you," I say choking on the salty tears streaming into my mouth. I finally let him go and see a huge wet spot on his shirt, "Sorry about that," I say pointing out the spot.

"No problem, I'm just glad you're safe," Raven said with a caring voice, still obviously affected by what happened to Miranda. "Hazel, are you okay?" He questioned while walking over to her shaking body in the corner.

"I just killed her, how am I supposed to feel," She sobbed, "I was trying so hard, I didn't want this to be true." Hazel was hysteric, and when Raven tried to get her up she crumbled in his arms. The door unlocked, and I went over to help Raven with the mess of a girl. We all exited the room together, everyone's faces turned to us.

"Where's Miranda?" Lexi squeaked, tears already forming in her eye's.

"I couldn't, I'm sorry," Hazel choked out, tears already running again. Lexi ran into her arms sobbing loudly, "shhh, it's okay, everything is going to be okay."

"Miranda!" Lexi's sobs continued for a while until she couldn't scream any longer. Everyone gave their condolences during her wailing.

"So this is real," Carmen whispered breaking the silence.

"Sadly," Raven replied.

"Sky are you alright?" Carmen questioned.

"I'm fine," I say in my normal monotone voice, keeping my guard up to keep safe.

"You are not just fine, you just about died how can you be 'fine'," Raven fired at me while flailing his arms angrily. He's cute when he's angry, but of course I can't say that I have to remain guarded and cautious, he can be the killer for all I know.

"Hazel are you doing any better?" I question to get the attention off of me.

"Yeah, I'm doing as good as I can, I mean I just watched someone die." She answered in sad voice. She seems to have become a mother like figure for Lexi, and Lexi has seemed to take a liking to her. With the emotional baggage hanging in the air we all somehow fell asleep.

"Huh," I say back in the pod, "I thought this was over." I look over to see Raven on the second puzzle again and Hazel struggling on the first one. The light turns on over the last table and Raven makes his way towards it, Miranda and Hazel fight with the exact same words as last time, but the air feels different this time. The walls erect around Raven again and everyone stops moving, not a single breath taken or released. The walls disappear as quick as they appeared and everything went black, the lights in the pods turn on again. A yellow gas seeps through the floor of the main room this time. "Nooooo," I scream as I see Raven and Hazel fall limp, the doors of the pods open and Miranda rushes towards me, and we run towards the door trying to get out, but the door doesn't budge. Miranda breathes in the noxious fumes, and falls limp bringing me down, and everything goes grey.

"Hey, Hey, Hey! Are you okay, you were tossing, turning, and you're sweating bullets," Raven says with concern while looking me over to see if there is anything else wrong with me.

"I'm fine, just a nightmare, I'm good," I say trying to keep my guard from crumbling around me.

"Come with me, I found a bathroom, We can get you cleaned up a bit," He says helping me up off the ground I fell asleep on. We went through the halls, and all I could pay attention to was the cracks and blood on the old walls. "Here we are," he says opening the door of the bathroom, "It's not in the best shape, but hopefully it will do." Raven sits me down on the toilet and runs a rag under some water.

"I'm fine," I say while trying to push his arm away, It doesn't work so I just grumble under my breath as he wipes down my face.

"You know you talk in your sleep," Raven said while rinsing off the rag in the yellow stained sink.

"I do, what did you hear?" I question hoping he didn't hear my whole dream.

"Nothing coherent enough to understand," He said with a shrug of the shoulders.

"Why did you help me, I could have done it myself," I ask but quickly covering up my confusion with coldness to keep my wall up

"I don't know, something just told me to help you, you seem troubled," He said with warmth in his voice. This boy is not what I need when a murderer is running around trying to kill us all.

"As I said before I'm fine, I don't need your help!" I say coldly trying not to let my emotions ,and problems breakthrough.

"Obviously you're not 'fine', just last night you were sobbing into my shirt after I saved you, then you have a nightmare that causes you to be screaming in you sleep. You're not fine you're going to have to tell someone what's going on, it helps,"

He yells, calming down at the end. I think about telling him, and I try to figure out how to start.

"Sorry to break up this beautiful moment, but you guys have to come and see this, Now!" Carmen said after busting through the door. She runs back out and we follow her through the old hallway. Once we reached the waiting room where we were all sleeping in I see Hazel and Mason on the ground screaming and hitting each other.

"You have no right to talk to that girl like that," Hazel screams landing a blow on Mason.

"That little girl deserves everything coming to her, she is a floozy," Mason yelled, "and so was her sister." I looked over to see Lexi crying in the corner, and Raven cooing her while raking his hand through her hair. I decide to rip Hazel off of Mason before the fight gets bloody.

"Let me go!" Hazel screamed flailing her arms wildly, "Let me at him!"

"Shut up! Both of you," Carmen yelled with a red face full of anger. She kicks her leg up letting her sparkling silver high heel fly off her foot. "Don't make me use this!" she exclaimed bending her knees holding the glittery shoe like a weapon.

"Woah, woah, woah, put that shoe back on your foot, and calm down." Raven said trying to calm down the hot-headed girl from stabbing someone with the shoe.

"Game Time!" The voice exclaimed, "everyone go upstairs to the second floor, and I will explain the game." We all looked around with fear and anxiety in our eyes, we all didn't move for a couple of seconds, then we all dashed for the stairway door. As we ran up the stairs the sound of heavy foot steps became present, and they weren't ours. We rushed through the door at the top of the stairs to be greeted by a tall ominous looking robot. "So here's the game, a simple round of hide and seek, but the first one to be caught will be eradicated, quickly followed by the lovely robot seeker," The voice said, "you have ten minutes to hide, and the robot has motion detecting vision so don't move, good luck." With that we all dispersed across the second floor of the hospital. I ran down the hall and yanked open the first door I saw, It was almost too dark to see anything in there. I saw a curtained off area, so I quietly fixed myself behind there making sure no part of me was visible.

"This is my place Sky, get out," the monotone voice of Carter scared me, but I couldn't see where her voice came from. "In here." A cabinet door across the room swung open showing the girl playing on her phone, "Now you see me, so find another room to hide in."

"Time's up, may your hiding skills be great enough to not be caught by my robot," The voice said.

"To late, now close that door and try to be quite, we can both get through this," I say with sureness. Carter just closes the door and I'm left in silence hoping nothing happens to me or Carter. My mind wanders to Raven, that boy is wonderful, so caring, nice, but I can't let him distract me from the murderer trying to kill everyone here.

"Grgg," My stomach growls loudly, " Crap, that was loud."

"Ya think," Carter said muffled through the cabinet. The sound of heavy steps grows louder, and then they stop

"I heard you," A robot says muffled by the closed door, then the door came flying in and hit the wall across the entrance. I shove my hand hover my mouth to quiet my breathing and to keep me from screaming out. "Don't worry I won't harm you," the robot said walking into the room, "Just kidding, I'm gonna kill you." I just hold my breath hoping it doesn't find me. I look around looking for an easy way to get out of here without being heard or seen, I see a closet and I shimmy my way over and into it silently. The robot's foot steps come near me, then going away, then come near me again. I hear the curtains being pulled back and I praise myself mentally for moving into the closet. The robot footsteps grow nearer, and the robot stops right in front of the closet, it's arm starts to extend towards the handle, but retro music blared from the cabinet that Carter was in.

"Crap, off off off," She said still monotone as always.

"Come out, come out wherever you are little girl," the robot says, his footsteps growing farther and farther away. I quietly peak my head out of the closet, and I see the robot approaching the cabinet. The robot stops in front of the cabinet and a wierd sound starts as it raises its arm up, then it kicks in the cabinet door.

"Ahhh," Carter screams then a bright light erupts from the arm of the robot. A huge blast sends me into the wall of the room, and everything just goes black.

Chapter 3.R

I hear an explosion from somewhere else on the floor , and I rush out of the cabinet of the bathroom I was in.

"What was that!" Carmen exclaimed while running out of the door right next to the bathroom.

"I don't know, I'm as confused as you," I say and we rush towards the sound that I heard. There was smoke pouring out of a room with no door, Hazel and Lexi turned the corner just as we arrived.

"What happened?" Hazel questioned out of breath.

"We don't know we just got here," I say, "maybe we should go in." Carmen grabs my hand and we go in together Hazel following behind, and Lexi staying out of the room. I see the door laying in the middle of the room and a lot of other random stuff on the floor.

"Who's that?" Hazel question pointing out a figure in the fog. I make my way over to the figure, and tears start to well in my eyes

"Sky," my voice shakes, "no please no." I shake his limp body hoping that my thoughts aren't true and he's still alive. The feeling I have for this boy have grown so much since being trapped in here, J always would just watch him walk around school just hoping for him to look my way or talk to me.

"Guhhh," Sky moans and starts to move around uncomfortably.

"Oh my god, Sky are you alright!" I exclaim with joy.

"I'm fine just a little scratch," He mumbles eyes still closed, I just slap him across the face, " hey what was that for." He opens his eyes to reveal the beautiful black orbs, and starts rubbing his face.

" That's for saying you're fine again, you are obviously not fine there is a hole in the wall right above you for pete's sake!" I yell, then I hug him a tear streaming down my eye. I help him up from the floor, "what happened?" I question once he was standing on his own.

"I came in here to hide, and I hid behind that curtain and the bed. The robot came in here because of my stomach growling, he kicked the door in too. I made the quick decision to get into the closet. He moved back the curtain and made his way to the closet, then," Sky choked out the last part of what he was saying tears streaming down his face.

"Then what?" Carmen pushed impatiently, "come on we need to know."

"Then Carter's game music started playing full blast, she was in the cabinet. The robot walked over to the cabinet raised its glowing arm, and kicked in the cabinet. Carter screamed then I was blown back into the wall, and everything went black," He just collapsed in my arms sobbing, and when he finished what he was saying the smoke cleared up a little bit. I looked to where he said Carter was hiding, and I was horrified at the sight of the dead girl. Half her body was charred, and there was a big sheet of metal through her side almost cutting her in half.

"Oh my god," I say pointing at the charred girl trying to keep my stomach down.

"Maybe we should just leave the room," Hazel choked out crying. We all leave the room, and I decided to carry Sky out as he didn't seem he could walk.

"What happened?" Dexter and Dan said in unison.

"Carter died," I quickly said trying not to create anymore tears.

"Oh," Dexter said shutting up after that.

"Why is this happening? What did we do to deserve this? Why did I come to this stupid, stupid, stu," Dan's breath became labored and he dropped to the floor in an anxiety attack.

"Oh my god," I say sitting down Sky, and scooting over to Dan's side,"Breathe, come breathe,"

"I can't, breathe," Dan heaves out his breathing worsening.

"This is only temporary, why don't we talk about your hobbies, what do you like to do?" I question trying to help out the poor boy.

"I like to, to play, chess," The boy said between heaves, his breathing slowing down slightly

"Me too," I say cheerfully, "What's you favorite piece?"

"The rook because it is the best piece," Dan says his breathing back to normal now.

"Hey Raven can I talk to you?" The now standing up Sky asked.

"Uhh yeah sure," I say getting up off the floor, and following him down the hall. We stop when we are out of hearing range of the others, when we stop Sky turns around to face me.

"Okay, this is a little awkward, but I want to tell you something I haven't told a lot of people." Sky says looking at me in the eyes.

"What is it," I say surprised, as he seems to be a very reserved person.

"The nightmare I had last night wasn't just a one time thing, I have them almost every night, its called D.A.D. or dream anxiety disorder," he explained.

"What exactly does that mean?" I ask confused on what exactly his disorder does to him.

"It puts me in a life threatening position during my dream, or having me actually die," He answers.

"Oh, well thank you for telling me," I say pulling him into a hug, "I hope I can maybe help you with these nightmares."

"No problem," he says pulling away from the hug, "It's the least I could do after you saving me yesterday and helping me twice today. There is a way you can help me, but it is a little weird to ask someone to do," He scratched his neck awkwardly

"Well what is it?" I question

"Well umm, it helps when someone sleeps in my bed with me, my parents used to but the don't anymore," He finishes, and my cheeks heat up from the awkward, but cute request. "So can you do that, I totally understand if you can't," He blabbers.

"Of course I can do that, anything to help you," I say quickly to try and stop his blabbering.

"Thank you," He says pulling me into a tight embrace, I hug back with the same firmness and we just stand there hugging. After a while we break from the embrace and just stand there in the comfortable silence. "Can I try something, and you have to promise you won't hate me after it?" he asks

"Yeah," I say hoping that he wants to do what I think he's going to do. He looks me In the eyes, then he looks slightly down, leans in, and kisses me. Sparks fly through my body, and I kiss him back for a few seconds until we part.

"You kissed back," Sky says surprised, and I just look at him and smile.

"Yeah to be honest I've liked you for about, I don't know six years," I say scratching my neck awkwardly.

"Wait really," Sky said surprised, "I have too, ever since I moved to Depsy, but I didn't think you even knew I existed.

"This is so weird because I thought you didn't know I existed," I said cheerful and surprised. We both started laughing, and we fall backwards together, and we fall into the bathroom that was behind us.

"Ahhh," Sky screams, and I just look over to what he was looking at and I'm horrified. I see a dead Mason with an indent in his head and a hole through his neck, fresh blood still pouring out of the hole.

Chapter 4.5

"What's wrong?" Carmen asked running into the room, "Oh my lord," She said, and just walked out it of the room touching her hand to her head, stomach, left shoulder, then her right shoulder. Everyone else rushed into the bathroom where the dead Mason lied.

"Someone is trying to compete with me huh," the voice said with a hint of bitterness, "I can't have this can I." We all look around each other anxiously waiting to hear what the voice plans to do. "I want Sky, the only one I know didn't do it, to figure out who did this horrid deed so I can deal with them myself," the voice finished and all eyes were on me.

"How do you know I didn't do it?" I question hoping to make the murderer crack a little.

"Oh baby, I have this place lined with cameras, besides bathrooms of course, and since you were in the room with Carter I know it wasn't you, And may I say you were so close to dieing weren't you." I just stay quiet after the answer I got. "So I want you all to go to the third floor where there is a common room and rooms for all of you," The voice says, "and there is food in each room." With the mentioning of food we all race up the stairway into the third floor.

"Where's the food y'all?" Dexter questions looking around the huge circular common room, he see's his name on a door and rushes into the room. "Oh sweet glory of Mac'n'cheese, get your cheesy goodness into the pits of my stomach," we hear Dexter yell. We all go to our rooms, and right before I enter Raven yells my name.

"What?" I ask from across the room.

"Bring your food to my room ok," I just nod in reply to Ravens reply. I enter my room, and I am wowed at how nice it is, there is a huge king sized bed, a desk with a pen and paper, and bookshelves filled with books covering the walls. I grab the meal left for me, and I make my way over to Raven room. I knock on the door, and It is opened instantly by the boy I have become so attached to. "That was quick," he said, "come sit," he grabbed my free hand and pulled me onto his bed.

"So why did you want me to eat with you?" I ask hoping for a certain answer.

"I don't know, maybe I wanted to kill you," he said tickling me, "but really I just wanted to hang out with you." A ring comes from my pocket, and I grab my phone that has a new message from a private number.

'I want you to start investigation tomorrow' -private

'Ok' -self

My phones screen became covered in code, then when it cleared up the conversation and all traces of the number was wiped from my phone.

"What was that?" Raven asked.

"The killer wants me to start investigation tomorrow, and then the conversation wiped itself of my phone," I explained.

"Oh, well do you think you're ready to do this?," Raven questions.

"Yeah, I just hope I don't mess up," I say with a hint of anxiety.

"You'll get the person, I believe in you," He encouraged.

"It's been years since I've done a murder case, so I'm a little bit rusty," I state.

"What?" Raven choked out, "you've investigated murders, what else have you done that I don't know about?"

"Uhmm well, I reopen and solve closed cases for fun, the last case I did was about a year and a half ago, and it turned out to be another murder from the Hook Murderer." I explained trying to clear things up for him.

"Hook murderer?" he questions.

"He's a killer that would bash in a vital body part of their victim then stab them through their throat or chest," I explained

'Oh, how about we talk about something else," Raven suggested shifting uncomfortably. The light all shut off and the door loudly locked.

"Goodnight guest, don't let the murder bite." the voice said.

"Well I guess we should go to bed," I say already scooting up the bed.

"Yeah," Raven says right by my side. I snuggle closer to him, and close my eyes hoping that my nightmares won't come back tonight. "Goodnight Sky."

"Goodnight Raven," I say, and with that I doze off into a peaceful sleep.

"Good morning, may all of you report to the common room for further instructions and investigation, "the voice says and the door unlocks.

"Ready?" Raven asks grabbing my hand, and squeezing it.

"Yeah as ready as I can be," I say, and we exit the room together hand in hand.

"Everyone except Sky will sit in a chair in the middle of the room until Sky makes a decision, I have taken pictures of everywhere accessible before the murder and the murder scene for Sky, and I have supplied a notebook and pen. Good luck Sky I hope you will find the murderer," The voice finishes and everyone except me sits in one of the chairs in the middle of the room.

"Okay let's start with the interrogation," I say standing in front of all the possible suspects. "I want everyone to tell me where they hid during the last game starting with Lexi going down the line," I finish grabbing the notebook supplied for me.

"I was in the farthest bathroom from the stairs to the left," Lexi stated.

"And I was in the bathroom next to the room she was in," Hazel said.

"I was in farthest doctors office to the right," Dexter says munching on some candy bar.

"I was in that bathroom to the right past the room you were," Raven said

"And I was in the doctor's office behind the room you were in," Carmen added.

"I was in the doctor's office to the left," Dan said.

"Okay and two individual questions," I say, "Dexter do you know how the robot heard me."

"No why would I," he replied.

"How about you Dan," I point the question towards him.

"I can't remember any of that game, I blacked out," He stuttered.

"Okay that's all I need mingle amongst yourselves," I say walking over to the pictures. I examin the murder scene again, he seems to have had his head bashed in by a rod of some sorts then stabbed in the neck with a smaller cylindrical object. I look at the faucet and it has splotches of blood on it, and it is big enough to have been the item that Mason's head was bashed in with. The wound on Masons neck seemed to be caused by something like a hook, this whole murder seems to be a Hook Murderer killing. I look at the floorplan of the hospital, and map out all possible routes from the hiding spots and the murder scene. "One last question and this is for the murder," I say walking back in front of the suspects.

"Yes, what's your question?" the voice asks.

"Did we all have the same meal, if not what did everyone have," I ask my question and wait for a reply.

"You all had the same dish, why is this relevant?" the voice asks obviously confused.

"Well with that I have discovered who the murderer is," I say proudly.

"Who?" everyone says leaning in.

"The Hook Murderer a.k.a. Dan Lowell," I say pointing my finger at the shaking boy.

"What, I didn't do it," The shaking boy starts violently shaking then falls limp on the floor. He jolts back to life, and jumps off the ground like a cartoon character that just came back to life. "Hello world, fill me in on what I missed," The boy with a now deviously whimsical voice said.

"What the hell is wrong with you! "Carmen exclaimed looking warily at the crazy boy. Everyone has now gotten out of their chairs a gained a little distance from the boy.

"Who me?" He asks with a hand on his chest like he was offended by what she said, and she just nodded. "Well to answer you question, nothing darling. I might have lost a couple marbles here or there but nothing to major," He said with his jolly demeanor never fading.

"Dan you can stop now we know you did it," Raven said approaching cautiously.

"Did what, and who is the Dan character?" He questions obviously confused.

"You're Dan, and you murdered Mason," Carmen said getting frustrated.

"Oh I get it, you think I'm the other guy in my body, no no no. I'm Quinn Shamble or as most people call me 'The Hook Murderer'," Quinn explained

"So you have Dissociative identity disorder, don't you," I say, "and you killed Mason not Dan, so that would explain why he blacked out and couldn't remember the game."

"Correct, and that prick Mason deserved what came to him, in the bits and pieces I saw of him he seemed like a worthless piece of scum," He said matter of factly.

"Wait this isn't the first time you've seen us," Carmen said confused.

"No sugar bun I have seen you guys at least three times in this hellhole," He stated.

"When?" Lexi shyly asks

"When I arrived here, when Mason and feisty brunette over there were fighting, and during that hide and go seek 'game'," He said.

"My names Hazel," Hazel said fire in her eyes already.

"Hazel, interesting, I would have thought something more like Courtney or Rachel," Quinn said. "Oh, and Sky don't think I don't know about you," He said, his demeanor changing to a dark and terrifying one replacing his past happy and jovial one. "You were the one who has tried to find me for the five years, you were the one who made me stop because of fear of being caught, it's always you," He starts to approach me slowly.

"Get away from him you psyco," Carmen says running in front of me with her shoe in her hand again.

"What are you gonna do you worthless girl," He hissed at her. She swung at him with her shoe and it stuck into his arm, he staggered back and ripped the shoe out of his arm and throwing it to the side.

"I hate people trying to meddle with plans!" He exclaimed and hastily made his way over to me leaving a trail of blood behind because of the stab wound. He grabbed me by the neck and dragged me to the window, "How about I just end you here, that would be fun wouldn't it, hahaha." His maniacal laugh ringing in my ear, I feel hand grab my arm and yank me away from the deranged boy.

"How about we do that to you," Carmen says ramming into the boy sending him out the window, he hits the parking lot with a crack and blood starts to exit the back of his head.

Chapter 5.R

"Are you alright? Did he hurt you?" I asked frantically hoping that he wasn't hurt by the deranged boy.

"Yes I'm fine and he did not hurt me to bad maybe a bruise around my neck, that's all," Sky said checking for other injuries.

"Fine, again with the fine!" I exhale angrily and get ready to slap Sky across the face, but a hand stops me from doing so.

"Calm down lover boy, he just about died give him a break," Carmen says trying to calm me down, but I just rip my arm out of her grasp and storm off murmuring profanities.

"Hey how are you doing?" I ask Hazel all calmed down by now.

"I don't even know how to feel about anything anymore, everything is just so crazy, first Miranda, then Carter, Mason, and now Dan who's next, Me?" Hazel says with anxiety and fear in her voice.

"I don't know, I don't want it to be someone I care about, but I care about everyone," I finish and we just sit there in silence waiting for someone to say something. Everything was silent except for the fear filled breaths taken by everyone in the room.

"Food is in the cafeteria on the first floor, but it's a game. See you there," the voice said, then everyone slowly made their way to the cafeteria. It was hard to walk down the stairs because all I could think about was the four lives that were taken by these 'games'. We arrive to the cafeteria, and there was a huge monitor and six desks with a sheet of paper on each of them. "This game is a trivia challenge, get a question right you get the right ingredient, get it wrong you get the wrong ingredient. Who ever gets the most wrong will get a dash of poison in their meal, have fun." The monitor flashed on and it said take a seat, when we all were all sitting it showed the first question.

" One, In the year 1900 in the U.S. what were the most popular first names given to boy and girl babies? A, William and Elizabeth B, Joseph and Catherine C, John and Mary," the mechanical voice of the monitor said. I scribble down my answer, and look around me only to see everyone stone faced and ready for the next question. "Two, Which of these is not to be found in the powder commonly known as 'Chinese five-spice'? A, Dill B, Cinnamon C, Cloves," The silence is broken only by the scribbling of pencils. "Three, In Greek mythology, Medusa was said to be what type of beast? A, Hydra B, Gorgon C, Basilisk. Four, Which of the following gases is produced from reacting magnesium with hydrochloric acid A,

Carbon dioxide B, Hydrogen C, Oxygen. Five, Who played Elle in the movie 'Legally Blonde'? A, Heather Graham B, Reese Witherspoon C, Renee Zellweger," I squirm a little in my seat because I love this movie. "Six, What magic power did King Arthur's scabbard have? A, Protected owner from injury B, Gave owner amazing strength C, Made owner invisible," The sounds of pencils dropping breaks my concentration, and I look up to see that the monitor says the quiz is over.

"Well that was fun, put your paper in the basket with your name on it and report to the kitchen," The voice that everyone knows all too well piped up. A door on the other side of the cafeteria opened, and we all dropped our paper off and went into the kitchen silently. "There are six mini kitchens, one for each of you. There are your ingredients and instructions for the recipe in the refrigerator of your kitchen, have fun cooking!" The voice cut off abruptly and we were left with only the music of our breaths to listen to. I walked to the refrigerator with my name on it, and started making the dish.

"Pasta Salad, I love this dish!" Carmen exclaimed sorting out her ingredients on the counter, "My abuela and I used to make this all the time." After that it went quiet, only the sounds of knives cutting and water boiling were present. Once I was done cutting all the ingredients and had my pasta in the boiling water I looked around to see how the others were doing. I saw Sky having troubles with cutting the tomatoes, his hair going everywhere, and his face filled with determination. Carmen was relaxing by her boiling pasta, obviously enjoying the experience. Hazel, Dexter, and Lexi's stations all reeked of bad ingredients, and they all look stressed out. Bubbles take me out of my thoughts, and I look over at my boiling water that is about to bubble over. I launch myself over to the pot and start stirring the noodles and water till the bubbles go down.

"That was close," I say to myself mostly.

"Yeah that was," Carmen says pouring her pasta into a strainer, steam puffing out of the sink. I follow her steps and strain out my pasta, then pour it into a big mixing bowl, and mix in all the chopped ingredients. I top off the pasta salad with Parmesan cheese and Italian dressing, then I put it in the refrigerator to chill for an hour.

"Once you're done you can go back into the cafeteria and socialize," The voice said and Carmen and I headed out of the kitchen.

"So how old is your abuela?" I ask her, as she mentioned her when we were cooking.

"She would be eighty-nine, but she passed away a couple of months ago," She replied with a hint of sadness. Sky entered the room with a smile and took a seat next to me and smiled at me.

"So what are we talking about?" He questions looking at both Carmen and I, his face morphs to concern.

"Nothing that's important," Carmen mumbled trying to avoid the subject.

"Well atleast we know we're safe, right," Sky said changing the subject.

"How so?" I question his logic.

"The murderer said that if you got a question wrong you would get a wrong ingredient, none of us had a wrong ingredient so were safe. The only people who have to worry are Hazel, Dexter, and Lexi," Sky finished, and it all clicked.

"Oh god, you're right," I say with worry, "Lexi's station smelled really bad, what if it's her, what if she dies?"

"At Least you'll be alive," Carmen deadpanned.

"You don't understand, you don't know her like I do, I was one there to comfort her after her sister dies, you weren't there! Also you didn't have to go through the pain of having your sister die, did you!" I scream at the top of my lungs, filled with anger and rage.

"Oh but I do know her, If you haven't noticed we all go to the same school, and live in the same town. She deserves to die, and so does Dexter, they are the worst people I have ever seen, just like every other person I have met. You two are the only people I have ever bonded with, and now you seem just like them," Carmen screams, and runs out of the cafeteria leaving me and Sky to soak up the words.

"She's right, you only are seeing one side of those two, they are a lot different than you think," Sky says and leaves to find Carmen, leaving me to my thoughts.

'Why are you so stupid, you do this every time, you should just end it now you ruined everything,' the onslaught of voices begins. I decide to try and find Carmen and Sky, but when I'm about to round the corner I hear Carmen sobbing.

"He just doesn't know them the way we do," I hear Sky say comforting her.

"They make fun of my skin color, and your sexuality, who does that?" Carmen questions between sobs.

"Horrible people, horrible people," Sky says

"I wish he knew what they say about him, if he knew he would understand the pain," Carmen says finishing her sobbing. I get up and walk back to the cafeteria with rage, I slam the door open to see Dexter, Lexi, and Hazel talking.

"Seriously, making fun of someones skin color, their sexuality. Thats low, and so stupid, we live in twenty-sixteen, you don't do that crap anymore," I yell pointing at Lexi and Dexter.

"Hey what's your problem!" Hazel exclaims getting in between me and the two I'm angry at.

"They're racist homophobic pieces of scum, I hiss.

"Where did you get that assumption from?" Hazel asks

"I overheard Carmen and Sky talking about it," I say trying to get Hazel on my side.

"Is this true?" Hazel asked turning around to face Lexi and Dexter.

"I only said those things because my sister said them," Lexi squeaked out on the verge of tears.

"Yeah I said those things, gays should burn in hell, and this country should have to deal with those illegal drug dealing latinos," Dexter says. Hazel punches one side of his face, and I get the other.

"Foods ready, if you don't get it right now there will be punishments," The voice said, seemingly trying to end the fight before it got to bad. We all scurry into the kitchen and grab our food from the refrigerators. "Also if you don't eat the food, there will be punishments for it," The voice said. When everyone got back to their seats Sky and Carmen ran into the cafeteria, and headed into the kitchen like there was a fire at their butts.

They ran back into the cafeteria and sat down trying to get their breath back.

"Lets eat," I said taking the first bite of food, everyone followed along.

"Wow it taste just like when me and my abuela made it," Carmen moans enjoying the meal she made. We all ate in silence then put our plates at the dish return window, even though there is nobody to take them.

"So does anyone feel weird, or poisoned?" Sky asks.

"I think they would be dead right now," Dexter said glaring at Sky.

"Can you back off or do you want another fist to your face," Hazel said getting in Dexter's face.

"I can take it, anyways you hit like a girl," Dexter said, but right before Hazel could hit him he started coughing. He fell to the floor wheezing, clutching his chest with his fist he choked out, "Help me," then fell limp.

Chapter 6.S

"He deserved that," Carmen said kicking the body just to make sure he was dead.

"Isn't it bad that you're happy about someone dying?" Hazel said, bewildered with how Carmen was acting.

"Next should be that little girl," Carmen said pointing her finger at Lexi, and narrowing her eyes into slits.

"I get it, they hurt you, but you don't have to go around wanting people to die," Hazel said getting closer to Carmen.

"No one understands the pain I've had to go through," Carmen screams socking Hazel in the jaw, Hazel just grunts in return.

"You really should watch who you start fights with because Raven and I dealt with Dexter and Lexi when you were crying somewhere because you couldn't deal with a little bit of pain!" Hazel screams getting in Carmen's face. "If you haven't realized other people have to deal with way worse things than a couple of mean things said to them. Miranda, Carter, Mason, Dan, and Dexter are all dead because of these stupid games, and guess what you're still alive. People of your race are killed everyday, and have to face the onslaught of hate for being suspected terrorist, and you get all hurt from being called a chola. Grow up, so many other people have worse problems than you, you should really think about that," Hazel finishes and just stomps off. Lexi follow quickly behind her leaving Raven, Carmen, and I in the cafeteria with a dead Dexter on the floor.

"So you 'dealt' with Dexter, what did you do, call him a name," Carmen sneered at Raven who just had a blank face.

"I punched him," Raven stated blankly and just walked out of the room.

"You need to calm down Carmen, you're gonna get yourself killed by doing this," I say trying to calm down the fuming girl.

"I want to get myself killed, don't you see that," Carmen says looking at me with watery eyes, "one of those three is the murderer, so I got them all to hate me so I get killed, can't you see that."

"I'm going to make sure that doesn't happen, I care way too much about you," I say with determination, "and where is that flare you had in the beginning of all this?"

"I don't know, dead, like everyone else," Carmen just gets up and walks out leaving me by myself. I make the long trek back to the third floor, and I knock on Raven's room door.

"Come in," Raven says. I walk into the room and take a seat on the bed, and just look at the boy laying in the bed.

"Are you ok?" I ask.

"I'm fine," he says turning away, and I lightly slap his shoulder for the response.

"You yell at me for using that word all the time, and now you use it," I say playfully trying to cheer him up.

"I'm not in the mood Sky," He says trying to end the conversation.

"Can we talk about this, I get that you and Carmen have become close in these past couple of day, and it hurts that she's acting the way she is, but she does this all the time. Carmen is a great person, but she's hot headed, and doesn't know when to close her mouth," I say rubbing his back trying to soothe him.

"It's not about that," He says turning around to face me.

"Then what is it about, you can tell me," I say reassuring him that it's okay to talk about his feeling with me.

"My depression has really kicked my butt today, I just don't feel like doing anything," He says adjusting himself into a sitting position.

"Wait you have depression, why didn't you tell me?" I ask wondering why he didn't tell me.

"I didn't think it was important," He states scratching his neck. I hear a clunk from outside the room, and I my detective instincts kick in.

"I'm gonna go get something from my room, I'll be right back," and with that I quietly open the door and exit the room. I see the stairway door close, and I decide to follow whoever was leaving to see where they're going. I open the stairway door, and I stealthily look over the rails of the stairs to see who it is, I see a hooded figure dragging what looks to be a body. I quickly and quietly walk down the stairs following the person, they go all the way to the first floor and leave the stairs. I exit the stairs, and see the figure crossing the room to the other stairway.

'What are they doing?' I question in my head. I quickly follow the person to the other stairway, and wait a couple of second before going in. I see the hooded figure walking down a flight of stairs that was not present in the other stairway. I arrive in the basement of the hospital and all I see is tubs and curtains and a pathway down the middle. I see the hooded figure drop the body and slap their face.

"Wake up," the person says, their voice muffled by something.

"Huh, where am I?" The voice of Hazel comes to my ear.

"Your death," The figure says, "any last words?"

"Who are you?" Hazel asks. The hooded figure takes of a mask revealing their face to Hazel.

"There now you know," A familiar voice says.

"I should have know it was you!" Hazel yells trying to get out of the killers grip.

"Well it's time for you to go," the killer says throwing the girl into one of the tubs.

"Aghhh!" Hazels screams are ring through the room, and a fizzing and popping noise in the background.

Chapter 7.R

I wake up to see Sky laying next to me, the morning sun on his face making him glow. He starts to shift round in bed so I decide to ask him a question that I have been wanting to ask," Hey where did you go last night?"

"I went to go get something that I lost on the second floor, when I got back you were asleep," He replies, his groggy from sleep.

"Oh ok," I say laying back down snuggling back into Sky, we just lay there in comfortable silence the rhythm of our breath and beating of our hearts synced.

"Good morning," The voice says, and Sky and I go to the common room ready for what's in store today.

"Hey I'm sorry about yesterday," Carmen apologizes walking towards Sky and I.

"No I should be sorry, what I said was uncalled for, and just plain rude," I say trying to get our friendship back on track.

"Where's Hazel?" The tiny voice of Lexi pipes up.

"Yeah where is that girl, I have to apologize to her," Carmen said.

"Maybe we should look for her," I suggest Sky squirms by my side, but I decide to shake it off.

"Yeah let's do that," Carmen says with a look of determination.

"Okay, Sky you check her room, Lexi you check the Second floor, and me and Carmen will get the first floor," I say, and we all leave to check our designated areas. Carmen and J arrive at the first floor, and a ominous feeling runs through my spine.

"What if she's dead?" Carmen asks with a hint of fear in her voice.

"Then she's dead, but let's not think about that," I say and we walk down one of the hallways. "You get that room and I'll get this one," Carmen nods and I enter the room. "Hazel are you In here," I say looking around, but I get no response and I don't see anything so I leave the room.

"Any luck?" Carmen asks.

"Nope," I reply, we continue on like this until we get to the other side of the floor.

"I guess she's not on this floor, let's go check on the others," Carmen says and we enter the stairway.

"Wait," I say putting an arm in front of her, "Is that a stairway down to a basement."

"I think it is, should we check?" She asks grabbing my arm.

"Let's go, she might be down there," I say and we start walking down the stairs. A vile smell hit my nose and I plug my nose to stop the sent from attacking my nostrils.

"What's that smell?" Carmen questions also plugging her nose. We reach the bottom of the stairs and we look around the room. "What's that?" Carmen asks pointing out a figure in one of the tubs. We approach slowly towards the tub, and when we get there a horrifying sight stains itself in our eyes.

"Oh my god, that's her," I say looking at her half melted off face, the rest of her body without skin.

"Let's go," I say grabbing Carmen's arm turning us around, but I see Sky with in the doorway with Lexi's wrist wrapped tightly in his hand.

"She did this, she's the one who has been killing everyone, I watched her last night kill her in cold blood.

"He's lying, he killed her, I swear I'm innocent," Lexi says tears welling in her eyes.

"That's what a murderer would say, you're the one who has been trying to kill us all," Sky hisses glaring at the little girl.

"Look at him, he's acting so scary, he's got to be the murderer," Lexi says in a baby voice, pouting.

"You have to believe me, she's evil," He plead with desperation in his voice.

"I believe you," Carmen says reassuring Sky.

"How about you Raven, do you believe me," Sky says with a sad look in his eyes

'He has to be telling the truth,' a voice in my head says.

'But look at her she couldn't hurt a fly,' another voice chimes in

'Don't judge a book by it's cover,' The first voice said

'That's true,' The second voice replied

'Sky's also a detective so I say trust him,' a third voice says, and I decide to trust Sky.

"I trust you Sky," I say looking at the boy.

"Oh thank god," Sky says with relief, "Now would you like to tell us why you did it, you little brat."

"Who me?" she says faking a cute voice, "How about not." Sky grabs the back of her neck and pushes her towards the tub with Hazel's corpse in it.

"How about now," She hisses holding the girls just inches away from the vile tub.

"Okay, okay I'll tell," She says and he releases her, but when he lets her go she switches spot with him pushing him towards the liquid.

"Oh no you don't!" Carmen yells knocking into the small girl.

"You think you'll win this fight, think again!" Lexi yells reaching up her skirt pulling a dagger out of her stockings. Carmen grabs her high heel and starts circling around in an old western duel style. Carmen charges at Lexi, but she is stopped by Lexi's dagger stabbing above her hip.

"Ughhh," Carmen's agonizing screams ring through the basement as she drops to the floor clenching the dagger.

"Ha, I told you, you wouldn't win, now that I know I'll survive I'll tell you why I'm doing this.

I'm trying to join the Frazen Cult, they are a group of murders who dedicate their lives to furthering the Jigsaw murdering style. This is my trial to get in, kill nine teenagers in many different 'games'."

"Why us though, what did we do to you?" I ask trying to make sense of all of this.

"I chose my sister because she was an annoying, dumb typical teenager that just deserved it, Carter Powell because girl gamers are so annoying especially when they have no personality, Mason Defain because even if I'm a murderer I hate bullies, Dan Lowell because I needed to get the other local murderer out of my way, Dexter Deter because I hate bigoted, sexist, racist, rednecks who think they own everything, Hazel Cras because people like her are just a bad image for America, Carmen Lough because I thought I would help her out with her wish of dying, Sky Masters because I needed to get rid of the detective prodigy who would eventually find me out, and lastly Raven Marett the perfect guy, good looking, smart, and a good guy, man I hate people like you." Lexi said stalking towards me.

"You get away from him you brat!" Sky yelled, but she just decked him in the face making him fall to the floor.

"I was wanting to kill you myself, to feel the life of someone so perfect drain from them, killed by a low life like me," Lexi said twitching. She screams and runs towards me, I quickly dodge the running girl, and she keeps going, running into a tub and falling in. "Ahhhh!" her screams fill the air along with the sound of sizzling skin.

Chapter 8.S

"Holy crap!" I exclaimed running towards the boy that just about got tackled into a tub full of acid. "Are you okay?" I ask checking to see if he's okay, he just nods, his eyes still wide open from the shock.

"Ugh!" I hear Carmen grunt, and I look back to see her with an empty stab wound, and a bloody dagger in her hand. "Got it," She says throwing the dagger on the grounds. "Ow, this hurts," She says clutching the open wound, she takes a piece of her shirt and dabbing it in the tub.

"What are you doing?" I ask in bewilderment.

"Sealing the wound silly," She says and wipes the wet piece of shirt on the wound, she hisses but she puts the two sides of the wounds together and wipes the wound again with a dry part of her shirt. "See," she says letting go of the wound, "sealed." I just look at her with bewilderment, and she just looks at me mouthing the word what.

"Lexi is dead, countdown started, traps set, only fifteen minutes to leave the hospital until self destruction," A mechanical voice says.

"Let's go!" Carmen yells and runs to the stairs, "Come on!" I grab Ravens hand, but he doesn't move he just yanks me towards him.

"Come on we have to g-," I stop at the sight of a rope wrapped around Raven pulling him up into the air.

"Help me!" I hear him scream, he struggles, and the rope starts to fray.

"Keep doing that," I say, but he stops above a tub filled with the acid, "Never mind, stay as still as you can, I'll try to get you down."

"Okay, but hurry!" Raven screams with desperation being the only emotion in his cry for help. I try to get the rope off him, but I realise that he's too heavy to lift by myself, and the rope isn't going to come off him unless it's cut.

"Carmen get the dagger and come over here," I look over to see her running with the dagger like a mad woman. Carmen starts to make quick work of the rope suspending Raven, and J try to hold him up so he doesn't fall into the acid.

"Almost got it," Carmen says biting her tongue in concentration.

"Ahhh," Raven screams as his foot is dunked into the acid, but I pull him out before anymore damage could be done. He blacks out and falls on the floor, Carmen and I wrap one of his arms around each of our shoulders and carry him to the stairs. We make it to the first floor and drop Raven heaving from the physical work.

"Five minutes remaining," The mechanical voice says, and we resume our trek to leave the building. I look behind us and see a yellow fog approaching.

"We have to hurry, toxic gas is coming our way," I say quickening our pace. I hear a clicking noise under my foot, and look down to see a bear trap ready to clamp on my leg.

"Come on Sky," Carmen says yanking me forward setting off the trap making an ear splitting sound emerge from my mouth.

"What's going on?" a groggy voiced Raven asked, he looks down at the ground and his face turns grim, "never mind, I remember."

"Carmen a little help." I say, but I see the girl running out of the hospital doors.

"I got it," Raven said getting on his knees opening the traps spiky jaws.

"Thank you," I say wrapping my arm around his shoulder, "let's get out of here." We limp out of the hospital together, the toxic fog close behind us.

"Oh my god, I'm so sorry, I went on autopilot and ran, I should have came back," Carmen said crushing both Raven and I in her embrace.

"It's okay, now let's get out of here," Raven says, and we both limp towards my car with Carmen trailing behind us. We get in and drive away, the just now rising.

"Where should we go now?" Carmen asks from the back seat.

"The hospital," I say eye's trained on road.

"Welco-," The receptionist say but stops because of our appearance, "I need doctors now!"

"What's the problem," A doctor says rushing into the room, "Oh my god, I need a big room cleared, Stat."

"On it," The receptionist says.

"What happened to you?" The doctor asks, and I tell him what has happened in the past few day. He rushes out of the waiting room and I grab Ravens hand and look him in the eye's

"We made it," I say looking him in the eyes, then he leans in and kisses me.

"We did," He says, I feel his smile on my lips, "and I found you, so it's all worth it."

"Hey don't forget about me," Carmen says pushing her way in between us, we just smile at each other in a comfortable silence.

"I love you both so much, I hope we never have to go through something like this ever again, I hope we can just live happily ever after," I say crushing the two I have grown so close to wishing

the moment would never end.